Published by Delacorte Press
Bantam Doubleday Dell Publishing Group, Inc.
666 Fifth Avenue, New York, New York 10103

First published in Great Britain by Walker Books Ltd., London

The trademark Delacorte Press is registered in the U.S. Patent
and Trademark Office.

Library of Congress Cataloging-in-Publication Data
Thompson, Carol
Time / Carol Thompson. p. cm.—(Primers)
Summary: Clocks show the time as a bear child goes through the
day from getting up, to school, and finally to bed.
ISBN 0-385-29765-3
1. Bears—Fiction. 2.Time—Fiction. I. Title.
II. Series: Primers (New York, N.Y.)
PZ7.T37/423T; 1989   88-18148
[E] — dc19   CIP
                                                              AC

Manufactured in Italy
First U.S.A. printing October 1989
10 9 8 7 6 5 4 3 2 1

TIME

CAROL THOMPSON

Delacorte
Press

The alarm clock rings.
What time is it?

It's seven o'clock.
Time to get up.

The oatmeal is ready.
What time is it?

It's eight o'clock.
Breakfast time.

Teacher's waiting.
What time is it?

It's nine o'clock.
Time for school.

Red. Blue. Yellow. Green.
What time is it?

It's ten o'clock.
Painting time.

Run. Jump. Hop. Skip.
What time is it?

It's eleven o'clock.
Playtime.

Bang. Toot. Ting-a-ling.
What time is it?

It's twelve o'clock.
Music time.

Yum, yum, yum!
What time is it?

It's one o'clock.
Lunchtime.

Hit the ball and run.
What time is it?

It's two o'clock.
Time for games.

Hello, Mom!
What time is it?

It's three o'clock.
Time to go home.

Warm bread, runny honey.
What time is it?

It's four o'clock.
Snack time.

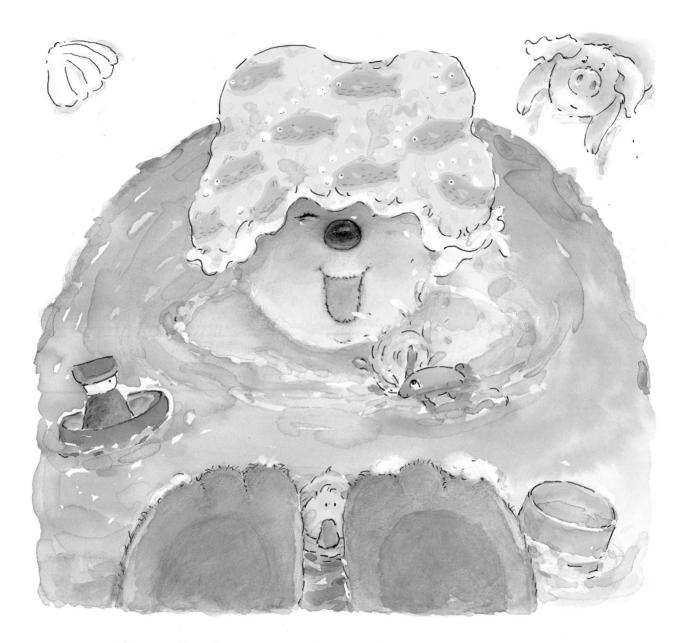

Splish, splash, splosh!
What time is it?

It's five o'clock.
Bath time.

After dinner, snuggle down.
Once upon a time...

It's six o'clock.
Bedtime. Soon to sleep…